FUN WITH
FASHION

Jeni Andrews

ASHTON SCHOLASTIC
SYDNEY AUCKLAND NEW YORK TORONTO LONDON

Section on hair written by Christine Pickup.
Section on makeup written by Lorraine Mehegan.

Photography by Ken Dolling.

Andrews, Jennifer.
    Fun with fashion.
    ISBN 0 86896 789 0

    1. Clothing and dress—Juvenile literature. 2. Cosmetics—Juvenile literature.
    3. Hairstyles—Juvenile literature. 4. Children—Costume—Juvenile literature.
    I. Title.

646.36

Typeset by David Lake Typesetting, Forresters Beach, NSW.
Printed by Canberra Press, Sydney NSW.

12 11 10 9 8 7 6 5 4 3 2   1 2 3 4 5 / 9

CONTENTS

FROM TOP TO TOE

You can have lots of fun experimenting with clothes, hairstyles and face paints. Invite your friends over for a weekend of creative busyness. Together you can update your old T-shirts, transform your sweatshirts into works of art, turn old business shirts into exciting new garments, create new hairstyles and transform your faces with different face paint patterns.

In this book you will find heaps of ideas for exciting clothes designs, sewing tips, hairstyles, face painting models, jewellery, accessories, all with simple instructions and making use of readily available materials.

So get ready and off we go on a creative whirl.

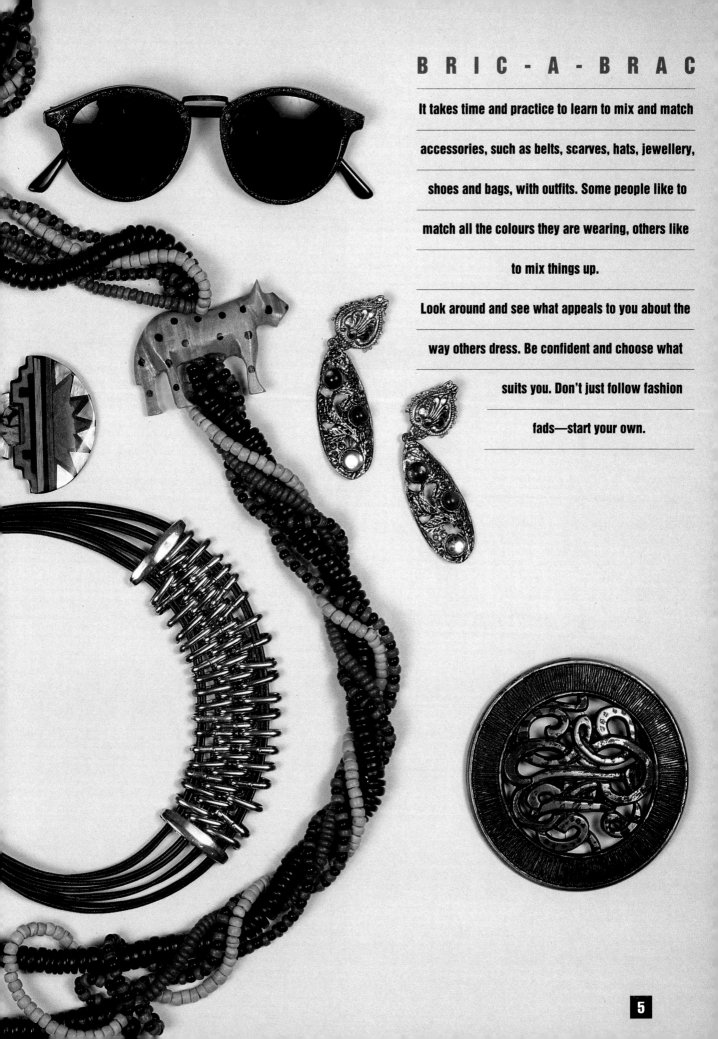

BRIC-A-BRAC

It takes time and practice to learn to mix and match

accessories, such as belts, scarves, hats, jewellery,

shoes and bags, with outfits. Some people like to

match all the colours they are wearing, others like

to mix things up.

Look around and see what appeals to you about the

way others dress. Be confident and choose what

suits you. Don't just follow fashion

fads—start your own.

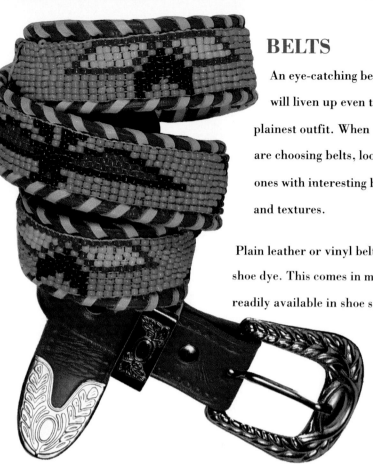

BELTS

An eye-catching belt will liven up even the plainest outfit. When you are choosing belts, look for ones with interesting buckles and textures.

Plain leather or vinyl belts can be repainted using shoe dye. This comes in many different colours and is readily available in shoe shops and drugstores. There are several different brand names to choose from. Make sure you follow the directions on the bottle carefully, for a really professional finish. You may change the colour of a whole belt, or simply use a small paintbrush to add colourful and detailed designs.

Use fabric paint or oil-based felt-tip pens to revamp fabric belts. Go wild! Liven up an old-fashioned floral belt with bright colours and some imaginative colour combinations.

Create belts with a Wild West feel by adding to them studs, fringes, braids and steel buckles. They'll look great with denim skirts and black jeans.

Scarves threaded through belt loops are a good alternative to belts. Twist together different coloured scarves, or thread chains or beads through the loops on your skirts, shorts and jeans.

For a touch of glamour, paste sequins or glitter onto plain plastic buckles. When you are creating designs with really fine detail, use tweezers to place sequins or other decorations in position.

BAGS AN

As well as protecting your eyes from the sun, sunglasses can add a touch of drama to any outfit. Don't let the current fashion trends dictate your choice of style too much. Try on lots of pairs and select glasses that suit your face.

Buy a cheap plain pair of black-rimmed sunglasses and use a fine paintbrush and enamel paints to decorate the top rims with small flowers, dots, stripes, hearts or stars. Do them all one colour or ring in the changes with a rainbow of colours.

BASKETS

Why not liven up your canvas backpack with a crazy design? You will need either oil-based felt-tip pens, poster paints or fabric paints. You will find plenty of ideas for designs on page 19. Draw on your backpack an outline of your chosen design in felt-tip pen and then colour it in with paint.

Decorate a favourite plain basket by attaching a posy of artificial flowers to one side. You will find wide selections of artificial flowers at craft shops.

Here are some other ideas to dress up baskets and bags:

- thread ribbon or lace around the handle, or through gaps at the top of the basket;
- pin badges and bits and pieces of jewellery onto a straw basket or fabric bag.

You can give a new lease on life to an old handbag, beach bag or any bag, with some creative decorations. Use shoe dye or fabric paints to create exciting patterns and designs on the sides. Sew or glue on sequins, lace, buttons or any decorative bits and pieces you can find.

Instead of using your new creation as a bag, store your jewellery, ribbons or scarves in it.

SUSPENDERS

Suspenders look great with pants and shorts. They are especially handy if you have a pair of pants that are too big in the waist. Buckle a belt tightly around your waist and attach suspenders. This will help hold up the pants and give a trendy bunched up look for baggy pants. Sew a few colourful buttons on the suspenders. Wear your suspenders with stretch Lycra pants or tights over a cut off crop-top. (See page 42 for crop-top ideas.)

GLOVES

If you live in a cold climate or head for the ski slopes in winter, you probably have gloves. A quick way to liven up a plain pair of gloves is to topstitch in brightly coloured yarn around the top of the gloves. Let the ends of the yarn dangle down and knot a bead or trinket onto the yarn. Use different coloured yarn to embroider funny little stitches onto the fingers.

Hats are becoming more and more popular. You can buy a new hat and jazz it up, or turn that boring hat you've been told will keep the sun off your face into a work of art. Other members of your family may have old hats they are willing to let you experiment on.

A quick and simple way to change the look of a hat is to tie a colourful scarf, ribbon or strip of material around the brim. For a more permanent effect, sew lace, ribbon or braid around the brim or crown of a hat.

If you want to change the look of an existing hat, simply fold the front back and stitch it to the crown. You may do this with any hat that is soft enough to fold back easily. Straw or felt hats are especially good for folding into unusual shapes. Use thread that matches the colour of the hat and make sure the stitches are neat. A double stitch in the centre of the brim should be enough to hold it in place. If you don't like sewing, use a small safety pin with a bow tied into it to hold the brim up, or pin it with a brooch or a badge.

CAPS

Baseball-style caps are very easily changed into eyecatching headwear. Ask your friends if they have some caps they no longer use. Or buy a very cheap plain one and let your imagination fly! Here are some ideas to get you going:

- make a crazy maze design out of assorted buttons—when sewing on the buttons be creative in your choice of colours of thread or yarn;

- caps also look great when dyed a new colour—just pop them in when you are dying a batch of other garments;
- fold the front of a cap back and paint a design on the part that is now showing at the front;
- pin badges and old brooches onto a cap or hat—you may have a collection of jewellery that you used to wear when you were a lot younger. Pin these onto the hat to make a 'memory lane'. This will be a great talking point with your friends.

S U N S H A D E S

Plain fabric sunshades can be brightened up by painting a surfing design on them with fabric paint.

S O C K S

Where do all the odd socks go? One sock always seems to be missing when you want it! Forget about trying to match colours. Deliberately wear different coloured socks. Wear two pairs at once and fold the underneath pair out over the top of the other pair. This look is fine for hiking, camping, fitness camp or sports. Try and co-ordinate your new sock combinations with the outfit you are wearing.

If your old socks are looking tired and faded, collect them all and re-dye them. You will have to experiment with the colours, as all the socks will be affected differently by the dye.

Another way to transform old socks is to find a variety of coloured yarns and sew them around the tops of the socks. Leave long pieces dangling down and tie a knot at the end of each one. You now have tassel-topped socks.

For something completely different, sew buttons up the side of your socks. You could match up all the buttons, or use a variety of shapes and colours and sizes. For a special party, sew sequins, ribbon or lace around the top of your socks.

For a floppy, scrunched down sock find some plain men's long socks and wear them bunched up over your ankles. These socks can also be dyed a more fashionable colour.

STRAW HATS

Straw hats are very easy to decorate with embroidery— you can use yarn or thread.

Sequins or beads can also be sewn on to create a glamorous look.

P A N T S

Jeans and shorts decorated with all sorts of fancy trims are very popular. However, these garments are very expensive to buy! A solution—buy a cheap plain pair and smarten them up yourself.

Decorative braids, laces and assorted trims are available at most fabric shops. To save money you might like to start a collection of interesting

trims, taken off old dresses, scarves and jackets. Hand-stitch the decorative pieces on your jeans and shorts around the edges of pockets, down the side seams, around the hem or the waistband.

Colourful patches of material may be fixed onto your pants. They may be just for decoration, or you might use them to cover a mark or stain. Maybe you ripped your jeans accidentally— cover up the tear with a patch. Bright bold colours or pretty pastel fabrics look good. Turn to page 46 for instructions on how to fix the patches on.

Brighten up a pair of jeans by painting a design on them with fabric paint. Use a fine paintbrush and put a design on the edge of your pockets. Dots and stripes formed into a pattern look good and are easy to do.

Some paints are available in bottles with a nozzle tip which enables the user to simply draw over the fabric. These are great for outlining or highlighting a design. They also come in glitter and dimensional (puffy) colours, which are sometimes called 'slick' paints.

Paint larger designs on the pockets or legs of your pants. Try outlining a flower pattern on the pocket—roses and daisies look good. Draw a simple outline using a laundry-marker pen or an oil-based felt-tip pen and then colour it in with paint. Highlight the centre of the flower with glitter or slick paint. For something different you might like to sew a few tiny beads or sequins in the centre. Why not use a glass or bead button?

Draw a cartoon character, stars and moon, hearts or strawberries on the legs of your pants or jeans. Trace the outline from a picture and then make a cardboard template to draw around. (See page 25 for tips on making templates.) Look in old colouring books or magazines for ideas.

WHITER THAN WHITE

Another way to change the appearance of denim is to use bleach. Ask an adult to help you and make sure you use only old clothes. Experiment with an old pair of shorts and jeans before bleaching something more important.

WHAT YOU NEED
- denim jeans or shorts to bleach
- old clothes or an apron or cover-up to protect your clothes
- rubber gloves to protect your hands
- a bucket
- 2 litre bottle of liquid laundry bleach.

WHAT TO DO
Wear old clothes and put on the rubber gloves before you begin. Empty the bleach into the bucket. Put the article you wish to bleach into the liquid and then cover it with cold water. Swish the article around in the liquid to mix the bleach and water together. Be careful not to splash any on your clothes, as it will take the colour out of them. Leave the article in the bucket for a few days for the colour to fade. Make sure to check regularly that any metal studs or zips are not going rusty. Some denims won't change colour very much, but others will become really light.

When your garment is the shade you want it, carefully empty the bucket into the laundry tub. Rinse the article thoroughly with warm water. To remove all traces of the bleach from the garment put it through the washing-machine cycle on its own, or wash it by hand.

Jeans can also be bleached using the tie-dye method. Before bleaching your jeans, twist them up and tie tightly in lots of places with string. Some parts will fade, others won't, so creating a pattern.

Tubes of glitter, pearly and slick fabric paint can be purchased in gold and silver plus many other colours. Use these to create a swirl pattern along the bottom of a skirt or the edge of a pocket. Put the same design on the collar or lapel of a jacket.

Hand paint a design as a border on a skirt. Choose a shape and repeat it around the hem. The easiest way is to use a felt-tip pen and trace around a cardboard template you have made of the shape (see page 25). Fill in the shape with fabric paint and then when dry, highlight details of the design with a fine paintbrush or nozzle tube— slick, glitter, puff or pearly.

DECORATIVE DESIGNS

SKIRTS

The fashionable length of skirts is forever changing. However, with the variety of styles now available, skirts can be worn long, short or in-between—gathered, straight or flared. Try and choose a style that suits your body shape. Miniskirts are back in fashion. A flared miniskirt looks great when worn over stretch tights that stop just above the knee.

A quick way to brighten up a skirt is to tie two centimetre wide ribbon, lace or braid into bows and then stitch the bows into position about two centimetres up from the hem. Sew them on with double stitches and try not to let the stitches show on the top of the bows. You could add just one bow or a whole lot.

Experiment by matching different colours, patterns and designs. For example:

- add spotted bows to a striped skirt;
- trim a black skirt with white or black lace bows;
- cut strips of fabric into ribbons and ask a friend with an overlocker to overlock the edges for you, then tie them into bows and attach to a skirt;
- put leftover pieces from the bows in your hair.

Plain denim skirts can be decorated using many of the ideas suggested for jeans and shorts. Other ideas include:

- stitch a daisy trim around the hemline;
- add the same trim to a top to make a matching outfit;
- trim clothes with gold cord, braid and other decorations;
- tie a shiny gold scarf or piece of gold fabric through the belt loops of your skirt.

GOLD ROPE

Make a gold rope to wear with your skirts.

What you need

2 lengths of gold cord, long enough to go around your waist, plus about an extra 40 centimetres.

What to do

Tie a knot in each cord, about 10 centimetres from one end. Twist the two lengths of cord together and tie another knot about 10 centimetres from the other end. Use your gold rope as a belt.

GOLD TRIMS

These may be stitched on your skirts around the hemline, on pocket edges or around the waistbands. They also look good on jackets, tops, jeans or shorts. Mix and match them to make different suits. You could replace the buttons on a top with gold ones to update it to match your skirt.

S H O E S

You can transform even the dullest pair of shoes

into a fashion statement using a variety of felt-

tip pens, fabric paints, shoe dye, and bits

and pieces of fabric.

LEATHER AND VINYL SHOES

You can change the colour of your ordinary shoes by using shoe dye, which is readily available from shoe stores and supermarkets. Follow the instructions on the bottle carefully and you will end up with a smart new pair of shoes.

To transform your shoes into something special for a party, sew or glue onto them gold braid, ribbon, lace or sequins.

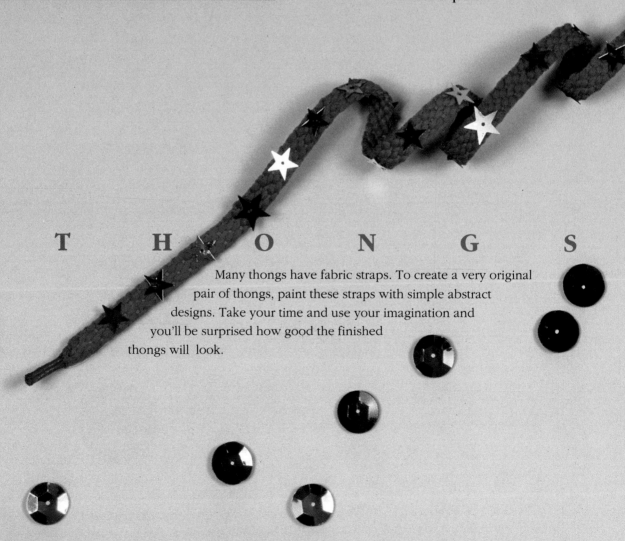

T H O N G S

Many thongs have fabric straps. To create a very original pair of thongs, paint these straps with simple abstract designs. Take your time and use your imagination and you'll be surprised how good the finished thongs will look.

These flat, cotton slip-ons are cheap to buy and comfortable to wear, and they are ideal for hand-painting. After a while these shoes tend to get rather scruffy, so paint a design over any dirty marks. To change their colour completely, just dye them the same way you would a T-shirt

(see page 26).

DECK SHOES AND SNEAKERS

Plain deck shoes and sneakers are one of the easiest items to decorate with fabric paint. You can paint a new pair or, if your old ones are looking tired and worn, give them a new lease of life by painting some exciting designs on them. If you are using new ones, you can paint directly onto the canvas with no preparation, but if they have already been worn you should wash and dry them thoroughly before you begin painting.

All sorts of designs look great on shoes, from palm trees, sun and surf scenes to spots, stripes and jelly beans. Match the colours with your favourite casual outfit. First outline your design in felt-tip pen and then colour it in with paint.

A quick tip: stuff the shoes with newspaper before you start and then they will be much easier to work on.

SHOELACES

There is no need to buy fancy shoelaces, you can create your own. Find a plain white pair of laces and then paint a design on them with fabric paint. You will have to use a very fine paintbrush, as the surface is so narrow. Or else try dyeing them a bright new colour. Just pop them in when you are dyeing something else.

You can also paint your old shoelaces, write names on them, or if they are stained draw patterns on them using felt-tip pens. And if they are dreadfully dirty, dye them a different colour.

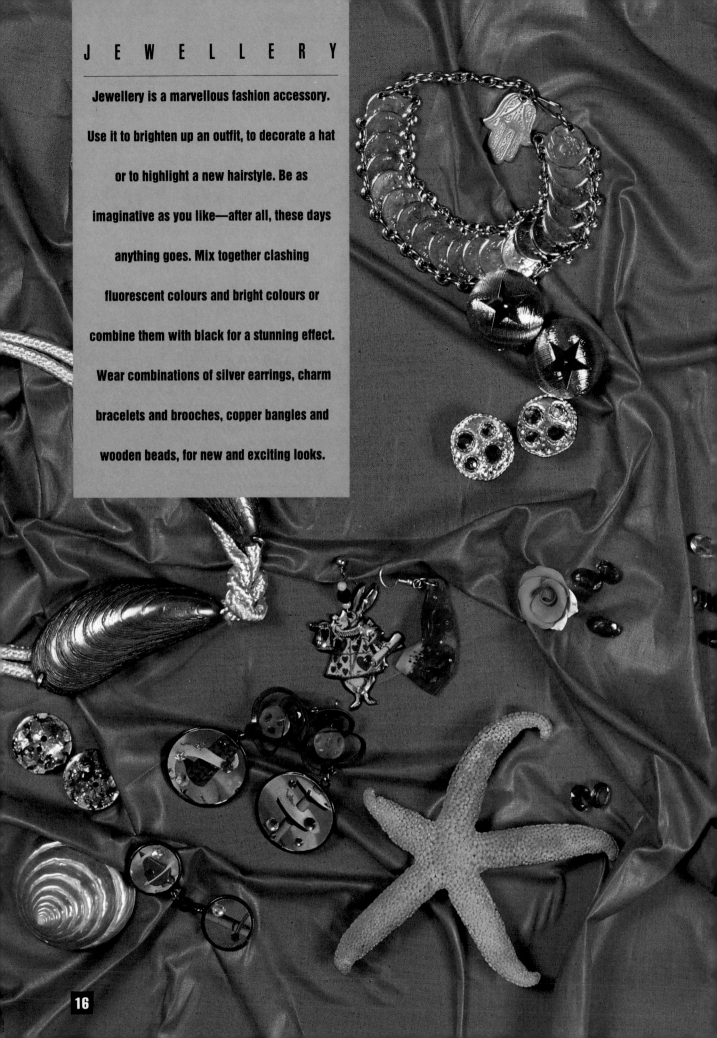

J E W E L L E R Y

Jewellery is a marvellous fashion accessory.

Use it to brighten up an outfit, to decorate a hat

or to highlight a new hairstyle. Be as

imaginative as you like—after all, these days

anything goes. Mix together clashing

fluorescent colours and bright colours or

combine them with black for a stunning effect.

Wear combinations of silver earrings, charm

bracelets and brooches, copper bangles and

wooden beads, for new and exciting looks.

Buttons, bows, crystal, beads, paint, clips, hooks and string can be used to create new jewellery or to jazz up bangles, brooches or earrings you may already have. All the bits and pieces necessary to make your jewellery are available from craft shops or can be collected from around the house.

Here are a few suggestions you can use to make your own jewellery, or you may be inspired by them to think up your very own ideas.

RIBBON NECKLETS

■ Tie a piece of velvet or shiny ribbon around your neck and pin or clip a sparkling piece of jewellery onto it for a party, dance or special occasion.

Earrings

■ Thread glass or wooden beads onto your sleepers or gold ring earrings to liven them up.

■ Paint plain plastic or wooden earrings with simple designs such as spots and stripes. Special wood and plastic paint is available from craft shops. Make sure you follow the instructions on the bottle carefully.

Necklaces, bracelets, anklets

■ Create exotic necklaces and bracelets by threading beads, large and small, onto string, fishing line, plain chains, thin elastic (hat elastic) or narrow strips of leather. Most of these necklaces, bracelets and anklets can be finished off by knotting the ends together at the back. Make sure you cut the thread long enough to go over your head, your hand, or your foot. Elastic is ideal for bracelets as it will not fall off your wrist.

■ Any object with a hole can be threaded—coins, trinkets, shells, seeds. A small hole can be made in shells by carefully twisting a needle around in one spot. Knot artificial flowers onto threads or attach them to clips for a decorative effect.

Tip: when using fishing line as a thread, ask an adult to heat-seal the knot at the back with a flame so that it does not slip undone.

BANGLES

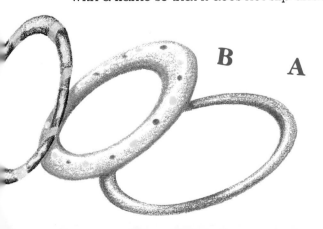

■ Plain wooden bangles can be painted with craft wood paint. These make lovely gifts for friends and relatives. Decorate them with colours you know they like. You could make a scarf to match the bangle.

BROOCHES

- Scatter pins are tiny brooches that are worn in groups of two or three. Try and pick a theme to group them together. It could be animals—but don't put a cat and mouse next to each other, you know what could happen! Flowers also look nice in a cluster.

- Ask friends and family to buy scatter pins for you as gifts for birthdays and Christmas, so that you can make a collection.

- Wear your scatter pins on clothing or pinned to a hat, socks, gloves, a scarf or a belt.

BADGES

- Transform largish buttons that have a rim around them into badges. Choose a picture you like, maybe a pop or movie star, or a photo of a friend or your pet. Lay the button over the picture and trace around it to get the right size. Cut out the picture and glue it onto the button. When the glue has dried, seal your badge with a coating of clear nail polish. On the back of the button fix a safety pin with a strip of strong sticky tape or super glue.

- Update any badges you have by covering them in the same way.

- Wear your new badges clustered together on the lapel of a jacket or shirt.

Make your own jewellery

- There are quite a few different brands of moulding material for jewellery available on the market. Fimo is one of them and is ideal for making necklaces, bracelets, earrings, badges and brooches. You can mould Fimo into any form you want, just follow the instructions on the packet.

- **Choose a theme of wild animals to create a whole set of jewellery from Fimo. Buy clips and pins as fasteners. Set safety pins into the back of your Fimo creations to make brooches.**

INSPIRATIONS

Here is a broad range of design ideas. Use it as

a source of inspiration for painting clothes,

jewellery, hair accessories, outfits and face

painting. ■ Pick a theme and use it to

co-ordinate different outfits.

T O P S

Transform a boring T-shirt, sweatshirt or top into an exciting garment using paints, dyes, ribbons, buttons, patches and all sorts of trims. Use your imagination when choosing designs and patterns. Look in colouring books, picture books and magazines—trace or copy the pictures.

- When using fabric paint always allow each coat of paint to dry properly. This can be done quickly but carefully with a hair dryer, or you may prefer to leave your garment on a flat surface until it is dry.

- When the painting on your top is dry, you will have to iron it to 'set' the paint. Use a hot iron and press over the inside of the garment slowly and carefully. This will stop the colour from washing out.

- Some types of nozzle-tube paints don't need ironing to set them, check the instructions on the tube. If you have used ordinary fabric paint first and then highlighted with one of the tube paints, be sure to iron your first paint work before applying the highlights.

T - S H I R T S

Screen-printing is an excellent way of putting a picture or pattern on a T-shirt. It is especially good if you have a large design.

You will need a stencil of your chosen design and a 'squeegee' with which to rub the paint through a mesh screen (see page 28). If you are a beginner at screen-printing, it is best to keep your shapes fairly simple, for example words or letters:

A variety of fabric paints can be purchased in bottles with a nozzle tip. They can be drawn over a fabric in the same way as can a pen. These are available in lots of colours and in glitter, pearl, puff and slick finishes.

You may like to use a combination of printing, hand-painting and nozzle tubes in one design. If you choose a daisy design, for example, the petals can be screen-printed, the centre of the flower hand-painted and the stem, leaves and petals outlined with a puff paint pen. The tubes are also good for adding spots and fine details.

Try painting a freehand design. You could start at the shoulder and just paint whatever comes into your head, or decorate around the neck edge then gradually work your design down the front. Pretend you are 'doodling'.

Make a special Christmas top for yourself or as a gift for a friend. Paint a Christmas tree shape on a top and use glitter, puff and pearl pens to decorate the tree. Add little stars and baubles in bright paint. Sequins, beads or pretty buttons can be stitched on the tree as well.

T-shirts and cotton tops are very easy to dye different colours. If you want to dye a top a plain colour just follow instructions on the bottle. To create a patterned effect on a T-shirt tie-dye it.

SHIRTS

Shirts may also be decorated like T-shirts and sweatshirts. You can paint on the collars, cuffs, pockets, back yokes, down the front openings where the buttons go.

Replacing plain buttons with bright, colourful ones, is an easy way to make a top more interesting. Try using different buttons instead of matching ones. Sew a collection of about six buttons up near the neck edge on one side. All sorts of crazy buttons can be used for this.

Sew around the hemline on the edge of the sleeves with coloured yarn or thread. Use large, straight stitches. Do two rows in matching or different colours. Start and finish with double stitches (see page 45). If you know any fancy embroidery stitches, add these as well. If you don't, ask someone to show you a few simple stitches or get a book out of the library.

VESTS

- To update a plain vest, sew a strip of fringe around the bottom.
- Change any buttons to gold ones, or add some bright ones if there are no buttons.

21

SWEATERS

Woollen sweaters look especially good with decorative stitching on them. On a fine woollen sweater use thin yarn or embroidery thread. For thick sweaters, use thick yarn. Create a design by stitching under and over the knitting to form a pattern. The stitches can be big or small.

Winter can be very dull, so be brave and use bright colours for your stitching, for example use navy, green and yellow yarn to liven up a red sweater.

Another simple idea: sew two rows around the bottom of the jumper and cuffs just above the ribbing. Leave about 10 cm extra hanging at the start and finish. Tie these bits together into a double knot. Just let them hang—a tassel! Knot beads or buttons onto the end if you wish.

S W E A T S H I R T S

These can be printed, hand-painted and dyed in the same way as T-shirts. Sweatshirts are easy to work on, as they are thick and don't move as you work on them as do some lightweight garments. Create a new design by cutting pieces of printed fabric into simple shapes. For example, cut out two or three squares of fabric, then cut pieces of double-sided interfacing (available at fabric and craft shops) to the same size. Peel the backing paper off one side of the interfacing squares and iron the squares on to the fabric squares until they stick together. Decide how and where you are going to place the squares on your T-shirt. Peel the backing paper off the other side of the interfacing, position the squares on your sweatshirt and then iron them in place. Outline the edges of the squares with a slick paint pen, to stop the fabric edges from fraying. Draw lines with paint between the squares to make a pattern.

Once you have practised this technique a few times, be more adventurous. Cut interesting shapes out of fabric, such as stars, flowers or animals. A fabric that has a floral pattern can be cut into a flower shape. Use Christmas material and try the ideas suggested for making a Christmas T-shirt (see page 20). Cut the material into a Christmas tree shape or a square, and decorate like a present. Paint or sew a bow on the top.

Here are some other suggestions:

- Dip a toothbrush or comb in fabric paint. Flick with your fingers to create a 'splatter' design. Use lots of bright colours. Wash the toothbrush after each colour.
- Rub paint through a piece of wire mesh with a toothbrush.
- Use a sponge or scrunched up tissue to blot on a pattern.

These methods can be used on their own, or mixed with other ways of applying paint to make a very textured look.

Lots of people wear big jackets or blazers over jeans. These can be expensive to buy, so why not see if you can find a suit coat no longer in use. Ask family members and friends for old jackets, or go to a second-hand clothing shop. Old school blazers also make good jackets. Navy and black are very popular colours but beige, grey or white can look smart, too. Change the buttons if you don't like the ones already on the jacket. Jazz up the breast pocket by hand-stitching a piece of braid or ribbon across the top. Pin badges or jewellery onto the collar. If the sleeves are too long, just roll them up!

P A I N T I N G

GENERAL HINTS

- Don't use too much paint.
- The paint should not be thick and lumpy, as it has to dry completely before you can wear your garment.
- Practise first on a piece of fabric or an old garment.
- Wash your brush in water after using each colour.
- Dry your brush on cloth before dipping into another colour.
- Paint may be dried with a hair dryer, put in the sunshine, or just left to dry naturally.
- When you have finished painting the garment and it is dry, iron it thoroughly before washing it.
- If you are using nozzle-tip pens for painting, practise first.
- Iron hand-painted areas before adding glitter, puff or slick decoration paints.

HAND-PAINTING

What you need
- fabric paint—bottles or nozzle-tip pens
- paintbrushes—thick and fine
- water
- clean rags.

It is easiest to work on garments that are stretched out flat when hand-painting and screen printing, so use a cardboard backboard or stuff newspaper inside the garment and tape it to a bench.

FABRIC PAINT

Fabric paints may be bought in small or large containers in all sorts of colours from craft shops and art material suppliers. You can buy just one colour to start with, or the three primary colours—red, blue, yellow, and black and white. By mixing these colours together, you can make many different colours. For example:
- mix blue and yellow to make green
- mix red and yellow to make orange
- mix red and blue to make purple
- for lighter shades just add white.

Experiment with different colours to make new shades. Pour the colours you have chosen to mix into a saucer or bowl. Always start with the lightest colour first and then add the darker shade, little by little. Store your newly created colours in jars with lids.

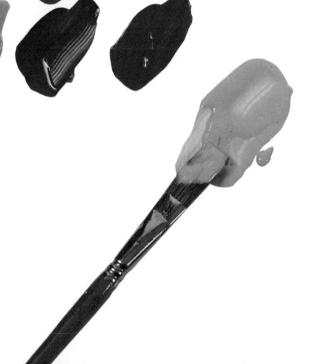

Make sure you keep your primary colours clean by using a clean spoon for each colour.

CARDBOARD BACKBOARD

What you need

- large piece of strong cardboard
- pencil
- ruler or tape measure
- old material or sheeting
- tape
- felt-tip pen
- scissors.

What to do

Use the ruler or tape measure to measure the length from the shoulders to the hem of a T-shirt or sweatshirt. Then measure the width from side seam to side seam. Draw a rectangle with these measurements on your piece of cardboard. Cut the cardboard to size.

Fold the material in half, and with a felt-tip pen draw on it a rectangle 28 cm longer and wider than the cardboard rectangle. Cut the material around the pen line to create two rectangles.

Lay the cardboard in the middle of one piece of material and place the other piece of material on top of it. Fold the corners in neatly—as you would do when covering a book. Tape the material together firmly on the back of the board.

Use the backboard when screen-printing and hand-painting a top.

TEMPLATE

What you need

- cardboard
- scissors
- carbon paper
- design/shape.

What to do

Draw your design onto a piece of cardboard. If you want to use a tracing of a particular design or shape as a template, trace around the picture first and then put a piece of carbon paper between your tracing and the cardboard. Draw around the outside of your tracing to transfer it to the cardboard. Cut out the shape with scissors.

Place your template on the garment you wish to decorate and draw around it.

DYEING

Always ask an adult to help you.

What you need
- bottle of dye
- large saucepan or washing machine
- apron
- gloves
- tongs
- plastic bag
- string or yarn if tie-dyeing
- salt.

What to do

There are many different brands of dye that can be bought from craft stores and art suppliers. Rit is a reliable and easy dye to use. Follow carefully the instructions on the label.

Garments may be dyed in a large saucepan on top of a stove or in a washing machine. The top of the stove method gives the best results, as the water can be kept hot.

Hints
- Add 1 tablespoon of salt to the dye pot to help hold the colour.
- Always wear rubber gloves and an apron.
- Use tongs when lifting garments out of the dye.
- Put the garments in a plastic bag to carry to the laundry for rinsing.
- Add salt to water when you wash the dyed article.
- Always wash the garments you have dyed on their own, so that they don't mark other things. Some dye may come out each time they are washed.
- White or pastel fabrics dye best.
- The more a batch of dye is used, the weaker the colour will become.
- Make sure you buy good quality dye.

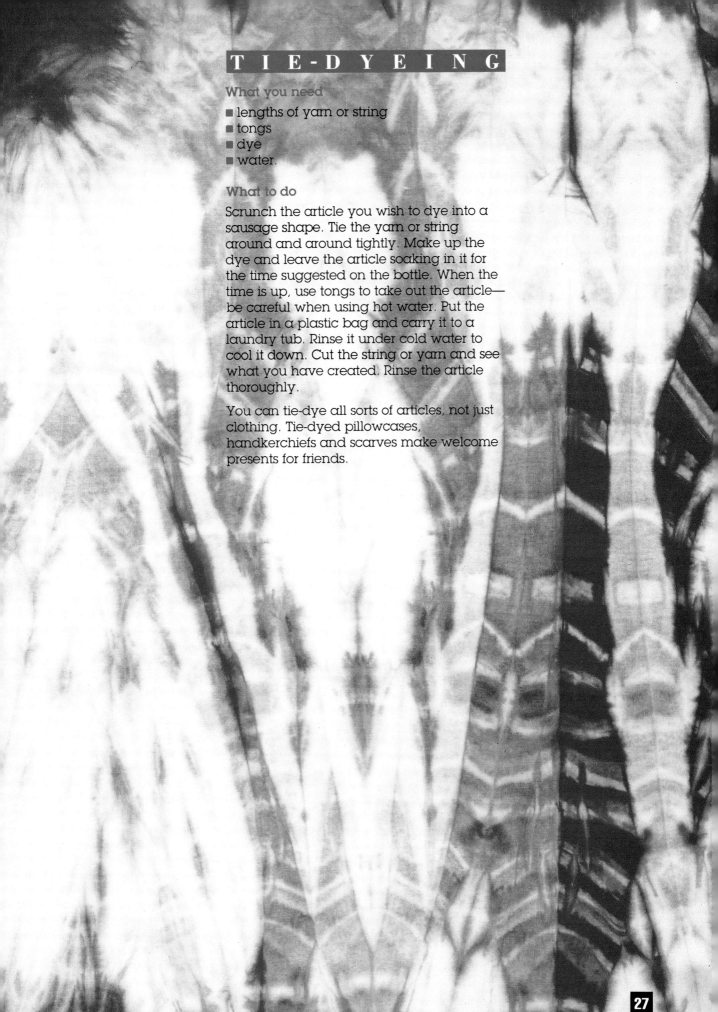

TIE-DYEING

What you need

- lengths of yarn or string
- tongs
- dye
- water.

What to do

Scrunch the article you wish to dye into a sausage shape. Tie the yarn or string around and around tightly. Make up the dye and leave the article soaking in it for the time suggested on the bottle. When the time is up, use tongs to take out the article—be careful when using hot water. Put the article in a plastic bag and carry it to a laundry tub. Rinse it under cold water to cool it down. Cut the string or yarn and see what you have created. Rinse the article thoroughly.

You can tie-dye all sorts of articles, not just clothing. Tie-dyed pillowcases, handkerchiefs and scarves make welcome presents for friends.

SCREEN-PRINTING

What you need

- stencil paper—you may use special plastic-coated stencil paper, newspaper, or butchers paper
- craft knife
- masking tape
- squeegee—a rubber scraper to apply the paint
- screen
- fabric paint
- spoon
- newspaper
- clean rag
- simple shape/design
- an article to print on
- flat table or bench.

Where do you get the equipment?

All the equipment for screen-printing is available from art or craft shops. There are screen-printing wholesalers in the capital cities. Look in your telephone book under Screen Printing Suppliers. Some companies will mail the stencil paper to you, once you have arranged payment.

What to do

Each colour must be printed and dried separately.

1. Cut out your paper stencil (see separate instructions).
2. Put newspaper or cardboard backboard inside your garment. If you are using newspaper as your stencil, tape the top to your work bench to stop it moving (see instructions for making backboard).
3. Lay the stencil on top of the fabric.
4. Place the screen over the stencil. Important—make sure that all the fabric under the screen, which you do not wish to

print, is covered with paper. Tape strips of newspaper around your stencil if you have not made it big enough.

5. Mix your colour. Spoon the paint onto the screen just above the design. Just a few spoonfuls should do. It takes practice to judge how much.

6. Scrape the paint gently down the screen with the squeegee. Hold it at an angle of about 60°.
7. Do three gentle strokes down and then one firm stroke to remove excess paint. The cut area of the stencil should now be free of paint.
8. Spoon off excess paint left on squeegee and screen. Put the paint back into the jar.
9. Stand squeegee up on its wooden end away from garment.
10. Lift up screen and stencil carefully together from one end. Stencil paper should stick to the screen with the ink. Stand up screen away from where you are working.
11. Dry your print with a hair dryer or leave to dry naturally.

12. You can add your second colour when the first is dry.
13. Peel stencil off screen. If it is special plastic paper, wash carefully and lay between two towels to dry. If it is a newspaper stencil, you can possibly save it by laying it flat on a piece of newspaper to dry.
14. Wash screen thoroughly in a tub or use a garden hose.
15. When you have finished printing and garment is dry, iron thoroughly before washing. Iron before adding any glitter. Iron slick or pearly finishes. Iron before stitching on any fancy decorations such as buttons or sequins.

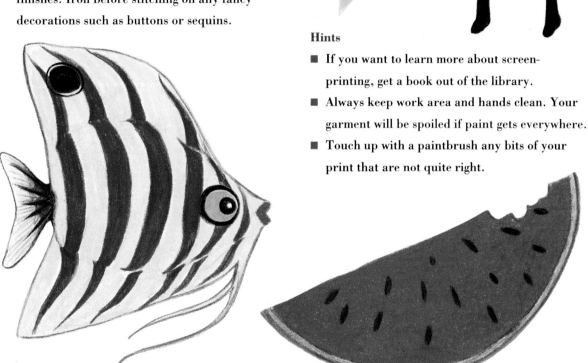

Hints

- If you want to learn more about screen-printing, get a book out of the library.
- Always keep work area and hands clean. Your garment will be spoiled if paint gets everywhere.
- Touch up with a paintbrush any bits of your print that are not quite right.

HOW TO MAKE YOUR STENCIL

The stencil is made by cutting from paper the shapes and areas you want to print.

- Keep your design shape simple at first, eg apple, star, square.
- Cut a piece of stencil paper two centimetres larger all around than your screen.
- Trace your design onto stencil paper by putting a piece of carbon paper between design and stencil. A simple pattern can be made by just cutting pieces of the stencil paper into geometric shapes.

- Place your design in the centre of the stencil paper or so that there are at least nine centimetres of spare paper around all edges. If you cut your design too close to the edge, paint will get everywhere when you print.
- Use a piece of thick cardboard as a base for cutting.
- With a sharp craft knife, cut away the parts you wish to print. Practise by cutting pictures out of newspapers.

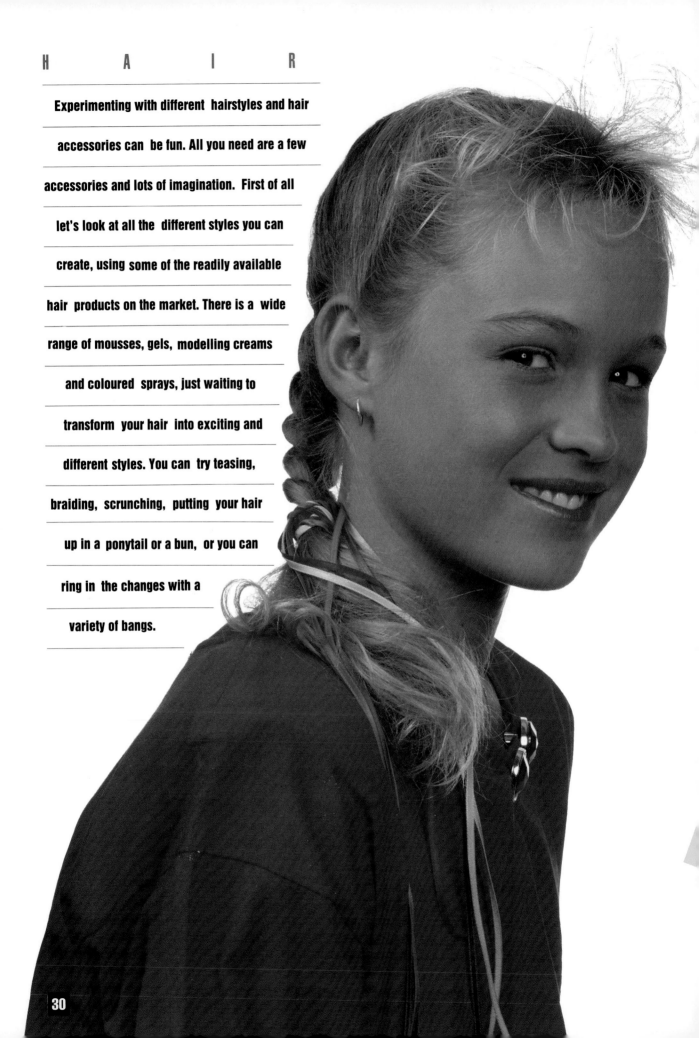

H A I R

Experimenting with different hairstyles and hair accessories can be fun. All you need are a few accessories and lots of imagination. First of all let's look at all the different styles you can create, using some of the readily available hair products on the market. There is a wide range of mousses, gels, modelling creams and coloured sprays, just waiting to transform your hair into exciting and different styles. You can try teasing, braiding, scrunching, putting your hair up in a ponytail or a bun, or you can ring in the changes with a variety of bangs.

BRAIDING

Braiding is easy once you know how.

Here are some suggestions for different styles you can create by braiding your hair.

■ Plait your hair into as many braids as possible. Tie long, coloured ribbons onto the ends of the braids, leaving the ends of the ribbons loose and hanging.

■ Plait braids all over your head or else do just one central braid down the back of your head.

■ Plait a circular halo of braids around the crown of your head. Start braiding on the left side of your head and wind the braid clockwise around your head. Finish your braid back where you started, behind your left ear.

■ Braid your hair and then wind the ends into a bun and secure with pins.

■ Thread fluorescent laces and ribbons through the centre of your braids.

■ Plait lots of braids all over your head—the more you braid, the more crinkly your hair will be when the braids are undone and the longer the effect will last.

■ To create a spectacular crinkly hairstyle, wash your hair at night and plait into a number of braids. Secure the ends with covered elastic—to protect them from splitting. Take the braiding out next morning. Remove one braid at a time and rake your fingers gently through the hair. Start with the underneath sections and work towards your face—this way your hair will tangle less. For special effects you can put your hair up in a high ponytail, or put half up half down, or try a high ponytail on the side of your head.

■ Alternatively, you could put your wet hair into a ponytail and then braid the ponytail and leave to dry. Take out for a crimpy effect. This way is quick and easy.

SCRUNCHING

Create a full fluffy look when you dry your hair by hanging your head over your knees and using your hair dryer on low speed and low heat. Run your fingers through your hair and lift out and scrunch the ends. To keep your new style looking good, either rub in a little mousse before you begin drying your hair, or spray the finished style with hair spray.

CRIMPING

To give your hair a lift for a special occasion, use a crimping iron to create soft, fine waves. Long, straight hair will look thicker and seem bouncier when it has been crimped.

COLOURED HAIR SPRAY

There is a large variety of coloured hair sprays on the market. Use them to give a basic hairstyle zing. You might like to match a colour to your outfit, or for special occasions try stencilling a design onto your hair.

- Draw a shape on cardboard, eg a diamond. Cut out the shape to use as a stencil. Hold the stencil onto your head, the side or back of your head is the best position, and then spray. This is easiest and more fun to do with a friend to help.
- Separate sections of a hairstyle may be sprayed, for example bangs one colour, ponytail another, or try striping your ponytail with two colours.

PARTY NIGHTS

Let your imagination run wild, try using coloured spray or glitter gel to create glamorous effects.

- Make up your own glitter gel by sprinkling glitter through a tub of clear gel.

SHORT HAIR

Use gels and mousses to create exotic and unusual looks. You might like to gel all your hair up and out from your head to get a spiky, messy look, or smooth it all back, leaving a few wisps out around your face.

A SHORT BOB

- For a change, secure your top hair from behind both ears with a scrunchie or bauble.
- Make a ponytail high on top of your head or pull it back under your crown. If you do this, try using coloured hair spray for an exciting effect.

TWISTING

To create an interesting twisted style, take a section of hair from each side of your head and put them behind your ears. Twist your hair in an anti-clockwise direction and push forward a little. Secure with pretty combs or clips.

PONYTAILS

High, low, teased, flat, scrunched or curled ponytails can be worn in a wide variety of ways.

- If you want to wear your ponytail at the nape of your neck, tie it in place with a lace, satin, or velvet bow.
- If your hair has been cut in layers, some of which don't reach into a ponytail, try a wet-look gel to hold it back.

BANGS

There are plenty of different ways in which to wear bangs.

- Scrunch dry your bangs.
- Curl them with a small round brush and a hair dryer.
- For a smooth look leave your bangs to dry flat.
- Roll the hair in your bangs under, or for something different separate individual bits with gel.
- Tease your bangs, then puff them up and touch them back off your face. You can hold them in place with hair combs or bobby pins.
- Use gel to smooth your bangs back or to make them seem wispy.

HAIR CARE

- All hair needs regular attention. If your hair is short it will need cutting more often, so that the style keeps its shape. The ends of longer hair, or hair all one length, need to be trimmed every few months.

- Have your hair properly cut at the end of every season. As the summer season is especially harsh on hair, it is important to remove damaged and split areas.

- Regular shampooing and conditioning will keep your hair in tip top condition. If your hair is inclined to be oily, put conditioner only on the ends; keep it away from your scalp.

- Brush your hair before you wash it, to remove excess scales and any gel or mousse.

- Always rinse chlorine or pool chemicals out of your hair after swimming in a pool. Do not let them dry in your hair, as this can cause hair discolouration and damaged ends.

- Eat plenty of fresh fruit and vegetables for shiny, healthy hair.

TEASING

Why not try teasing your hair? Use the fingertips and palm of one hand alternately, and rub your hair in circular movements. This will tease your hair at the roots and make it stand up. If you would like a curly look, scrunch the ends and then spray with a small amount of hair spray.

ACCESSORIES

Hair accessories are limited only by your imagination.

S C A R V E S

A scarf is one of the most commonly used hair accessories. It is not necessary to spend a lot of money on scarves, you can easily make your own out of a piece of material that may be left over after sewing an outfit—you will then have a matching accessory.

See page 44 for hints on how to collect interesting fabrics that could be made into scarves. If nothing suitable is available, buy half a metre of cheap fabric from a material or craft shop. This will usually make two scarves. Check the sewing instructions on page 47 for what to buy and how to make it.

- To brighten up a plain scarf, paint a design in one corner with fabric paint, or be more radical and cover the whole area.
- Cotton scarves are ideal for tie-dying!

Here are some suggestions as to how to wear your scarf:

- match it to an outfit headband style;
- around your ponytail;
- as a bandanna—twisted around your forehead—covering your head and tied at the back.

HAIR COMBS

Buy a few different coloured hair combs and decorate them yourself.

- Dried flowers may be woven on a wire and attached to a comb.
- Spread fabric glue on the comb and sprinkle with glitter for a sparkly effect.
- Stick stars across the top of a comb.
- Enamel paint is great to paint your own shapes and patterns and gives you a look all of your own.

SCRUNCHIES

What a name! Those bright tubes of material and elastic which are twisted around a ponytail can be made at home. Small pieces of material that have been saved can be used up in this way. Bright, shiny and see-through fabrics are great for making scrunchies. Sew sequins on the scrunchy to add sparkle. See page 47 for instructions on how to make your scrunchy.

If you have a skirt that needs taking up, cut off the excess hem and make a scrunchie—all you need is a piece of fabric, elastic and needle and thread.

R I B B O N S

Ribbons are a favourite hair decoration.

- Plain ribbons can be brightened up by having a design hand-painted on them. Any type of ribbon is suitable. If using nylon ribbon do not iron to 'set' the paint, as you will be told in the instructions. Just test iron a little bit at the end of each ribbon to see if it can be ironed. Mostly it is not wise to iron nylon. Do not wash the nylon ribbon once it has been painted.

- A few different coloured ribbons, plaited together and secured at the ends with needle and cotton, look good plaited through hair or tied around a ponytail.

Y A R N

- Cut three coloured strands (maybe six if it is thin yarn) into 30 centimetre lengths. Twist or plait them together. About eight centimetres from each end, tie a knot, thread on some coloured beads and tie another knot to finish. Use in your hair instead of ribbons.

- Collect different types of yarn from people who knit. They will always have bits and pieces left over. Mohair (fluffy) and yarn with shiny threads are especially good to use.

N E T T I N G

Netting, or tulle, the mesh that ballerinas' tutus are made out of, can be used in all sorts of ways to brighten up your hair.

- Tie a piece of elastic into a band big enough to go around your ponytail. Tie the netting into a double knot through the band to form a bow. This can also be done with any band you would normally use to keep your hair in place.

B A U B L E S

What you need
- covered elastic
- shank buttons—buttons with hooks underneath
- paint or glue and glitter.

What to do
Thread buttons on to elastic and then tie the ends together with a knot. The size of the bauble will depend on the amount of elastic you use. Paint the buttons your favourite colour, or else glue glitter on them.

C O M B S A N D C L I P S

Plain combs and clips can be transformed by using a little imagination. Here are a few ideas. You will think of many more!

- Sounds crazy—looks great! Cover the top of a comb or clip with craft glue and carefully shake multicoloured 'sprinkles' (yes, the ones you eat!) onto it. Cover the whole area. Put on a flat surface and allow to dry. A coating of clear nail polish can be added when dry. Try gluing glitter, tiny beads and sequins on. Great gifts for friends.

- Make your own padded bow—large or small—and stitch it to a bobby pin, band or clip.

Face painting can add a special touch to a party. A basic supply of paints, crayons and lipsticks will provide many hours of fun for everyone.

■ To create the best effect on your lips, outline them first in crayon and then apply the lip colour (either paint or lipstick). Next place a folded paper tissue between your lips and press down. Add some more lip colour and use the tissue again. Lastly, apply some clear lip gloss with a lip brush or your finger. If you really want to highlight your lips, then zinc cream in fluorescent colours is the best to use. Zinc cream will also protect your lips from the weather and will stop them from cracking.

■ If you want glitter or stars to stick to your face, apply some hair gel to the part of your face that you want to put glitter on, and then sprinkle the glitter onto the gelled area.

■ Apply a moisturiser to your face before you paint it, to stop the face paints from cracking. Paint the area of your face in the colour you want and then rub over very lightly with a hair gel or apply a face powder (it must be loose powder, not a powder from a compact).

■ In order to get the exact shapes you want on your face, practise first on paper and then use white chalk on your face to make the outlines. The chalk can easily be rubbed off if you make a mistake, or painted over if you are happy with your design. (It is easier to draw shapes on someone else's face than to do your own, so try sharing ideas with your friends.)

■ If you want to make the shapes you create on your face look neat, then you can make a template to use as a guide. To do this you will need some cardboard. Draw the shapes you want on the cardboard and then cut them out. When you want to make a shape, just place the cardboard with your shape over the part of your face where you want it and trace the inside of the cardboard with chalk or crayon outliners.

■ To give your face a smudged look, apply the paint with a dry cotton ball and brush over with talcum powder. Then use your fingertips to smudge the area on your face.

WHAT YOU NEED

- a face-paint kit—available from toyshops (most kits have the primary colours and you can mix up your own colours from these)
- a set of crayons for outlines—silver and gold are handy
- a lip crayon and some lipsticks—a gloss will give you shine
- zinc cream in a collection of fluorescent colours
- glitter
- a mirror
- ask an adult for any old cream eyeshadows you can use as paints (after applying these, pat the cream with a cotton ball dipped in talc to stop any wrinkles)
- ice-cube trays, or egg-cartons, in which to mix colours
- make-up brushes (make sure you have a thin lip brush for lips and tiny areas of work)
- hair gel is useful for smoothing the face paint and applying glitter
- a basin full of warm water to wash your fingers
- baby oil—to take off the paint
- cotton balls
- cotton swabs
- paper tissues
- talcum powder or face powder
- a suitable container to store all your paints, crayons, glitter, eyeshadows and zincs. The lids must be kept on the paints and zinc creams and all make-up should be kept out of the sun and heat, preferably in a cupboard
- a sharpener for large pencils—to sharpen your crayons (most make-up lines also carry these sharpeners).
- When using zinc cream, or cream eyeshadow, always brush over with a cotton ball dipped in face powder, to stop cracking and smudging.
- It is important not to get any paint, gel or glitter in your eyes, so be very careful when you apply make-up to your eyes. Use a small brush or a cotton swab. Your eyes are very sensitive to infections, so if you are going to share your paints with friends, always use a small spoon or spatula to take out the paint (never your fingers) and put it into an egg-carton or tray before applying or mixing the colour you want. Do the same with cream eyeshadow and zinc cream.
- Crayons can be wiped with a paper tissue and then passed to the next person to use.

WHAT TO DO

1. Tie your hair back off your face—use a shower cap or headband.

2. Tie an apron around your neck to protect your clothes.

3. Put moisturiser on your face.

4. Choose the design or look you want.

5. Select or mix the colours you need.

6. Use a piece of white chalk to draw outlines for practice.

7. Paint your forehead, cheeks, chin and nose first—allow them to dry. If you want to dry your face quickly, sit in front of a fan turned to low or use a hair dryer turned to low.

8. Do your eyes, lips and eyebrows next. Crayon works best on eyebrows.

9. Draw in chalk the shapes that you want on your face. Outline in crayon and use a thin brush, or cotton swab, to apply the paint, zinc or eyeshadow.

10. Apply glitter to your face while the paint is wet.

FLOWER POWER

paint face white or natural

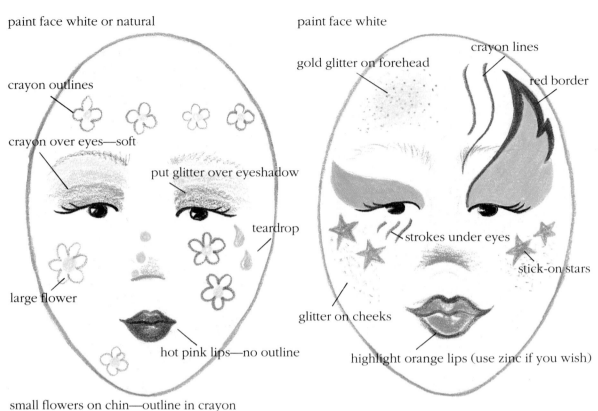

crayon outlines

crayon over eyes—soft

put glitter over eyeshadow

teardrop

large flower

hot pink lips—no outline

small flowers on chin—outline in crayon

DISCO DANCER

paint face white

crayon lines

gold glitter on forehead

red border

strokes under eyes

stick-on stars

glitter on cheeks

highlight orange lips (use zinc if you wish)

SPACE FACE

paint silver—sprinkle with gold glitter

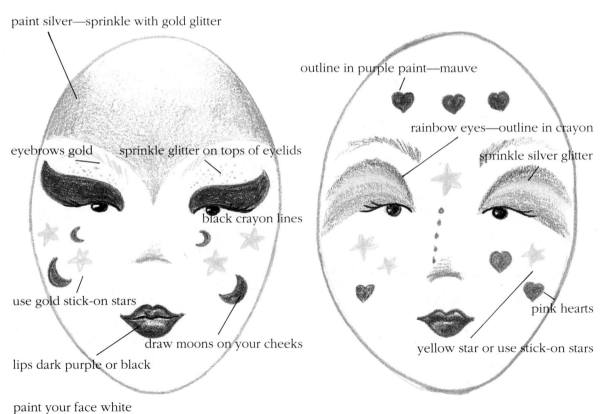

eyebrows gold

sprinkle glitter on tops of eyelids

black crayon lines

use gold stick-on stars

draw moons on your cheeks

lips dark purple or black

paint your face white

CARE BEAR KID

outline in purple paint—mauve

rainbow eyes—outline in crayon

sprinkle silver glitter

pink hearts

yellow star or use stick-on stars

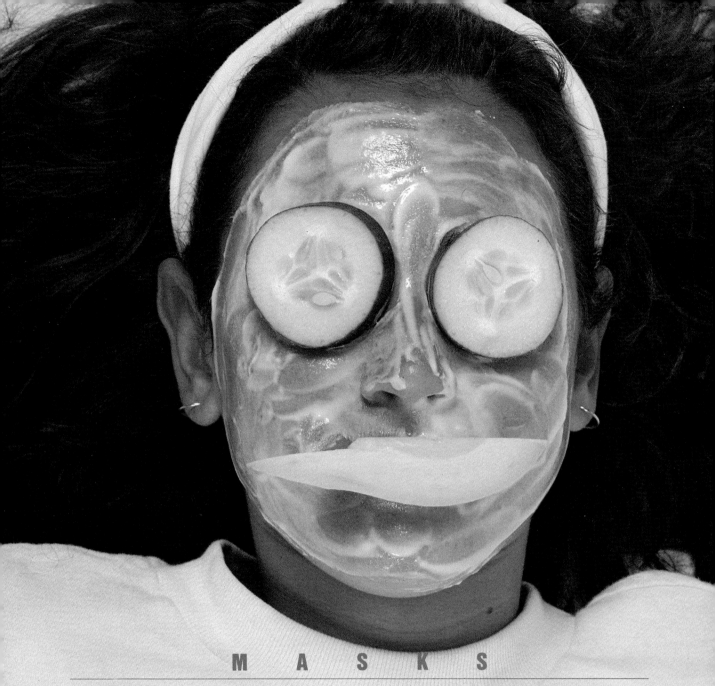

M A S K S

You can have a lot of fun using food on your face and at the same time give your skin a healthy lift.

FOOD FAVOUR

- Clean your face thoroughly and then smear yoghurt over it. Do not put it over your eyes and lips.
- Cut two slices of cucumber and put them over your eyes.
- Put two avocado slices on your lips.

MUD MADNESS

- Mix up some mud, smear over your face.
- Cut two slices of kiwi fruit for your eyes.
- Rub a cut strawberry into your lips.

SKIN CARE

- Always clean your face each morning and night, either use a natural soap or a mild cleanser. Rinse and pat dry.
- Wear a sun-screen on your face every day, especially in summer. A hat will protect your face from the sun.
- Use a lip balm to stop lips from cracking in winter and burning in summer.
- Never use pens, felt-tip pens or pencils on your face to create the designs.

There are lots of ways to update your old

clothes. If you look carefully around your home

you will find many bits and pieces you can use

to jazz up jeans, tracksuit pants, T-shirts, skirts

and sweatshirts and save them from the rag

bag.

SWEATSHIRTS AND T-SHIRTS

Transform your old sweatshirts and T-shirts into crop tops. Put on the garment you wish to change and then make a pencil mark at waist level. Take it off and then extend the pencil line around the whole of the garment. Leave the back a little longer than the front. Cut carefully around the pencil line with a pair of scissors. There is no need to hem the edge. Crop tops can be worn to the beach or pool, or over leotards to ballet or gym.

Old sweatshirts and T-shirts can also be painted, printed or dyed to give a new fresh look (see page 20).

SHIRTS AND BLOUSES

Old shirts and blouses are great to experiment on. Your family may have some you can use. Men's old business shirts are ideal for turning into new trendy garments, because they are usually big and floppy. Paint or decorate the collars, cuffs, backs and sleeves with fabric paints. Wear your new creations with the sleeves rolled up over a T-shirt and with jeans or shorts.

Old shirts make great painting and cooking cover-ups.

JEANS AND TRACKSUIT PANTS

Cut off the legs of old jeans and tracksuit pants to make shorts. To do this put them on and then make a pencil mark on each leg of the pants where you would like the new length to be. Take them off, lie them flat on a table and use scissors to cut straight across the mark you have made on the legs. There is no need to sew a hem as the ragged edges will give your 'new' shorts a casual look. Jeans can be frayed slightly by pulling at the loose threads around the edge.

If there are any marks or stains on the pants, use brightly coloured patches to cover them up. Cut the material for the patches into interesting shapes, pin them in place and then stitch them on. If you don't like sewing, stick the patches on with fabric glue or iron-on interfacing (see page 46).

SCARVES

Scrounge around for old scarves no longer being worn. Older female family members or friends might surprise you with some that have interesting patterns and designs. Look for ones with unusual textures and colours. To make a large scarf, simply sew several small ones together.

The scarves you find can be worn in your hair, through belt loops, around your neck or stuffed in a jacket or shirt pocket for extra colour.

The scarf fabric could also be cut up to make scrunchies.

Store your most precious jewellery and keepsakes in a silky scarf. Lay the scarf out flat. Put all your goodies in the middle and then tie the opposite corners together to make a parcel. Or just scrunch the scarf up around the bits and pieces and tie with a ribbon.

SWEATERS

Unravel old woollen, hand-knitted sweaters and roll the yarn into balls. Ask an adult to show you how to knit. Start with something simple, like a scarf. Another idea is to knit small 10 centimetre squares, using different coloured yarn. These can be sewn together with yarn to form a patchwork blanket.

Use the yarn to embroider different designs on socks, plain sweaters and T-shirts.

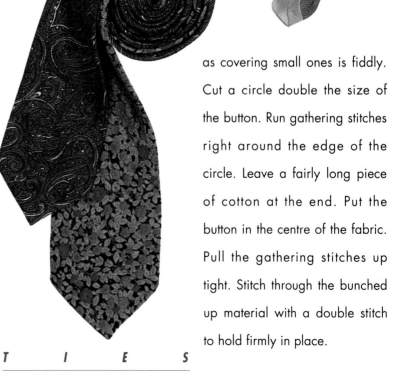

Ties come in masses of different colours, patterns and fabrics. Take the chance to collect any old ones that appeal to you. You can use the material to make scrunchies or to cover buttons. Kits for covering buttons can be bought quite cheaply from sewing shops, but any round button can be covered. It is easiest to cover large buttons, as covering small ones is fiddly. Cut a circle double the size of the button. Run gathering stitches right around the edge of the circle. Leave a fairly long piece of cotton at the end. Put the button in the centre of the fabric. Pull the gathering stitches up tight. Stitch through the bunched up material with a double stitch to hold firmly in place.

T I E S

If you have some old clothes you don't want to revamp, they still can be useful. Sort through them before you put them in the rag bag and cut off any buttons, buckles, trims (such as lace and braid), labels, interesting pockets and emblems. Once you start looking you'll be amazed at what you'll find. Start a collection of things that can be used to decorate other garments.

Labels can be arranged in a pattern and stitched by hand down the sleeve of a T-shirt or sweatshirt. Put them on the legs of shorts or jeans or on the front of a jacket. Double-sided interfacing can be ironed on to fix labels (see page 46).

Some garments may have lovely fabric which you can cut up into usable pieces, fold and save for later use.

Decorate an old pillowcase and use it to hold your 'bits and pieces' collection.

SKIRTS AND DRESSES

If you have a favourite skirt or dress that is too short, simply sew a lace border on the bottom to make it longer. If it is too long, cut it short into a mini skirt. Use the material you have cut off to make patches and shapes for other garments.

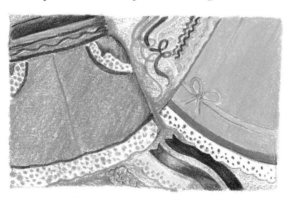

PYJAMAS

Old pyjamas have a lovely soft feel to them, because they have been worn a lot. If you can't bear to get rid of them, even though they are much too small, just cut them off in the same way as you change jeans and tracksuit pants into shorts. Winter pyjamas can be worn in summer as short pyjamas. Sew a lace trim around the edge of the legs and on the bottom of the pyjama jacket.

SWIM SUITS

If the colours of your swim suits have faded, brighten them up with fabric paint. To get a good result, stretch your suit over a strong piece of cardboard. Part of an old carton would be fine.

If the fabric is plain, your choice of design is unlimited —fish, sun, waves, boats, palm trees, zig zags.

But if the material is patterned, just highlight parts of the design with the paint.

Allow the front to dry thoroughly before turning over to paint the back.

Check the painting instructions on page 24 before you start.

SEWING INSTRUCTIONS

DOUBLE STITCH

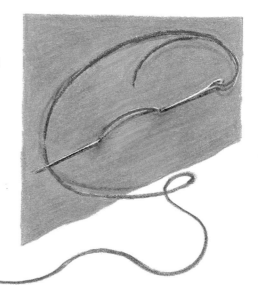

This strong stitch is used for fixing stitches at the start and finish of work.

1 Bring the needle through to the right side of the fabric from the wrong side.
2 Leave a little bit of thread at the back.
3 Make a small stitch backwards.
4 Bring the needle through again to where you started.
5 Do the backstitch over again.

This process can be repeated several times if you want to fix something on tightly.

RUNNING STITCH OR GATHERING STITCH

This stitch can be used for gathering or for sewing on trims, such as lace, braids, ribbon.

1 Start with a double stitch.
2 Work from right to left.
3 Take several small stitches onto the needle at one time.
4 Pull the needle through.
5 Do this again and try to keep stitches even in size.
6 Repeat to end of work.
7 Finish with double stitch.
8 If you wish to gather the material—don't do a double stitch at the end, instead leave about five centimetres of thread hanging. Pull the thread so that the stitches bunch up into a gather.

TOPSTITCH

Use this stitch for a decorative trim.

1 Make a double stitch.
2 Work from right to left.
3 Make even stitches about ½ cm long around the part that you wish to trim.
4 Finish your sewing with a double stitch.

HEMSTITCH

1 Start with a double stitch.
2 Work from right to left.
3 Use the needle to pick up one or two threads of the fabric.
4 Put the needle through the folded part of the hem.
5 Pull through.
6 Pick up another two threads from the fabric.
7 Repeat back into the hem fold.
8 Continue this all around the hem.
9 Finish with a double stitch in the fold.

BACKSTITCH

This is a strong stitch used for seams.

1 Work from right to left.
2 Do a double stitch.
3 Make a stitch backwards—about half a centimetre.
4 Next, bring the needle through ½ cm in front of your double stitch.
5 Do another ½ cm backstitch and bring the needle through ahead as before.
6 Repeat to end of seam.
7 Finish with a double stitch.

DOUBLE-SIDED INTERFACING —IRON-ON

A very simple way of attaching things to your clothes without sewing. Use it to fix on patches, fabric shapes, labels and trims to clothes.

What you need
- double-sided iron-on interfacing—available from craft or fabric shops
- iron
- pair of scissors.

What to do
1 Cut the interfacing to the same size as your patch.
2 Iron the interfacing on to the patch until it sticks.
3 Peel the backing paper off the interfacing.
4 Iron the patch to your garment.

SEW-ON PATCHES

1 Cut your patch to size.
2 Iron under one centimetre all around the patch. Make the corners neat.
3 Pin the patch to the garment.
4 Stitch by machine or hand, using small topstitches close to the edge.

SCARF

A good size to cut a scarf is 50 x 50 cm square—this should allow two scarves with most fabrics. Just change the scarf size, depending on the width of the fabric.

What you need

- ½ metre of medium weight cotton fabric
- pair of scissors
- needle
- thread
- pins.

What to do

1 Iron back a one centimetre fold all round the fabric.
2 Fold the fabric back another one centimetre to form a neat hem.
3 Pin all round.
4 Make sure the corners are neat—like you do when covering a schoolbook!
5 Stitch by machine or by hand—use hemstitch or backstitch.

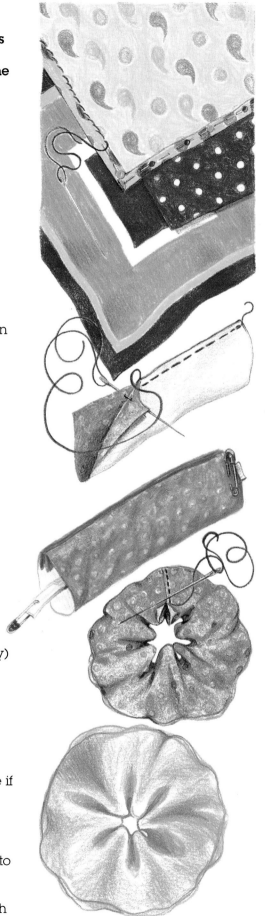

SCRUNCHY

For a medium-sized scrunchy.

What you need

- strip of fabric—40 cm long by 10 cm wide
- elastic—20 cm long by 1 cm wide (approximately)
- safety pin.

What to do

1 Fold the strip in half with right sides of the long edges facing each other.
2 Pin in place, so that the wrong side is showing.
3 Sew a row of backstitches ½ cm from the edge down the long side of the fabric. Sew by machine if you can.
4 Roll out the fabric to the right side.
5 Attach a safety pin to one end of the elastic.
6 Push through the tube.
7 Use lots of double stitches to attach elastic tightly to each end.
8 Put the two ends of the scrunchy together.
9 Stitch neatly and firmly right across the top of both ends.

INDEX